PLAYDATE PALS

KITTEN LEARNS TO LISTEN

Rosie Greening • Dawn Machell

make believe ideas

Kitten was good at lots of things.

She was good at painting . . .

good at playing games . . .

and good at singing.

But she wasn't very good
at **listening** to her friends.

One day Hippo said, "Let's paint!"
Kitten was good at painting,
so she started right away.

She was so busy that she **didn't hear** her friends decide to paint pictures of **themselves**!

Soon the friends stopped to look at each other's pictures.

Everyone had painted a picture of themselves except **Kitten** – she had painted a flower!

"Oh **Kitten**, remember to **listen**!" said Hippo.

After that, Puppy suggested they play a new skipping game.

"I like games!" thought **Kitten**, and she started to chase a butterfly.

But she was so busy running around that
she **didn't hear** Puppy explain the rules!

The animals started playing the game.
But **Kitten** didn't know how to play!

"Oh **Kitten**, remember to **listen**!" said Puppy.

Soon, Bear came in with a plate of cookies.

He said, "Do you want a cookie, **Kitten**?"

But **Kitten** was too busy singing to **listen**, so he walked away.

After a while, **Kitten** noticed the cookies.
She ran over, but her favorites were gone!

"Oh **Kitten**, remember to **listen**!" said Bear.

Kitten felt sad.
She kept **missing out** on things!

"I'm going to **listen** from now on!" she thought.

Later the friends decided to play dress up.

This time **Kitten** remembered to **listen**.
She reached the dress-up box first . . .

so she got to wear her favorite costume!

Kitten had lots of fun playing with her friends.

"I'm glad I **listened**!"
thought **Kitten**, with a big smile.

READING TOGETHER

Playdate Pals have been written for parents, caregivers, and teachers to share with young children who are beginning to explore the feelings they have about themselves and the world around them.

Each story is intended as a springboard to emotional discovery and can be used to gently promote further discussion around the feeling or behavioral topic featured in the book.

Kitten Learns to Listen is designed to help children learn about listening and paying attention to others. Once you have read the story together, go back and talk about any experiences the children might share with Kitten. Talk to children about listening and then encourage them to do so in other trusted relationships.

Look at the pictures

Talk about Kitten. Does she look happy when she doesn't listen? What about when she does listen? Help children think about the benefits of listening.

Words in bold

Throughout each story there are words highlighted in bold type. These words specify either the **character's name** or useful words and phrases relating to **listening.** You may wish to put emphasis on these words or use them as reminders for parts of the story you can return to and discuss.

Questions you can ask

To prompt further exploration of this behavioral topic, you could try asking children some of the following questions:

- Do you like it when people listen to you?
- When should you listen? Why?
- How could you make someone listen to you?
- What is good about listening?